Stories from the Heart of a Child

A Little Child Shall Lead Them

Faith Easter

WestBow Press books may be ordered through booksellers or by contacting:

WestBow Press
A Division of Thomas Nelson & Zondervan
1663 Liberty Drive
Bloomington, IN 47403
www.westbowpress.com
1 (866) 928-1240

ISBN: 978-1-5127-2970-2 (sc)
ISBN: 978-1-5127-2971-9 (e)

Library of Congress Control Number: 2016901829

Print information available on the last page.

WestBow Press rev. date: 03/29/2016

CONTENTS

CHAPTER 1

HAPPINESS IS CONTAGIOUS

Sarah was an orphan. She had lived at the orphanage in the village for two years but still had trouble making friends. All the other children would run and play while she sat with her doll, Molly, under the dogwood tree. The other children teased Sarah because she was a homely girl who never smiled.

One day as she sat under her tree, Mrs. Hampton, Sarah's favorite teacher, joined her. "Why are you sitting here by yourself, Sarah?" she asked. "I'm too sad to play." Sarah said. "The only friend I have is my dolly. She never makes fun of me. She likes me just the way I am." "I like you just the way you are too, Sarah, but do you know what would make you a very pretty girl?" "No. What?" "Well, first of all I think we should brush your long golden hair and put it in braids." "You would do that for me?" "Yes, Sarah, I would. You see, Sarah, I love you, and I want to help you find something to smile about.

Now go get your brush and we'll take care of that hair!"

"Okay, I'll be right back!"

A few minutes later Sarah was back with her brush and her doll's brush as well. "Would you put Molly's hair in braids too?" "Sure, then you can be twins." "That'll be fun, Sarah said excitedly." "Well what in the world is that on your face?" Mrs. Hampton asked. "Sarah looked into the mirror she had brought outside. "I don't see anything on my face!" "I do, Sarah. I see a great big smile!" With that she gave Sarah a big hug and Sarah hugged her right back. "It's time for me to go back inside. Why don't you see if you can play a game with the group of girls playing over by the basketball court." "That's a good idea," said Sarah, and off she went.

For the first time since she had been there, the others welcomed her with opened arms and Sarah had the most fun she had ever had.

The next day was beautiful. The sun was shining, the birds were singing, and the frogs were jumping in and out of a nearby pond.

Sarah didn't know when she got up how special this day would be. She dressed herself, brushed her hair, and put on her prettiest headband. At breakfast Mrs. Hampton sat with her. "Good morning, Sarah!" "Good morning, Mrs. Hampton!" Sarah greeted her. "Where's Molly?" "I decided to let her sleep in today. She played really hard yesterday!" "You had a lot of fun yesterday, didn't you,

Sarah?" "I sure did and I hope today will be fun too." "Today I have a surprise for you, Sarah." "What is it, Mrs. Hampton?" "Well, Sarah, there's a new little girl coming to live here and I thought you could help her get settled." "Oh, I'd really like that! What's her name?" "Her name is Brianna and she is three years old." "When will she get here?" "She will be here at ten o'clock." "Oh boy, I can't wait!"

When ten o'clock came, Sarah was sitting on the front steps waiting for Brianna to arrive. Soon she saw the blue station wagon coming up the long driveway to the house. "Mrs. Hampton! Mrs. Hampton! Brianna's here!" "Okay, Sarah, bring her into my office."

Sarah went back outside to find a little girl with Shirley Temple curls, walking hand in hand with a lady who looked much like an old school marm. She was tall and lanky. She wore her hair in a bun and had wire rimmed glasses. "Well hello there, sweetie! I'm miss Hutchins and this is Brianna with her favorite teddy, Max." "Hi. My name is Sarah. I'm seven and this is my favorite doll, Molly. I will show you where Mrs. Hampton's office is. She is waiting for you." "Okay, we'll follow you." They walked down the long corridor until they reached the last door on the right with Mrs. Hampton's name on it. They knocked on the door and went in.

"Here they are Mrs. Hampton. This is Miss Hutchins and Brianna." "Thank you, Sarah. Please wait outside while we take care of the paperwork, and then you can show Brianna her new room." "Okay, I'll sit on the bench in the hall."

It seemed like forever, but finally the paperwork was done. "Come into the office for a minute, Sarah. I need to talk to you." "Is something wrong?" "No, but I need to explain something to you." "Okay." Sarah sat down next to Mrs. Hampton and looked up at her with quizical eyes. "Sarah, Brianna smiles all the time and she giggles when you talk to her, but she cannot talk." "Why not?" asked Sarah. "Can't she hear?" "OH yes, she can hear and she used to talk all the time, but something happened in her family." "What happened, Mrs. Hampton?" "Her mother died and she thinks it's her fault. She went away and didn't come home and Brianna hasn't spoken since." "How did her mother die?" "She had to stay in bed for many days and finally she had to go to the hospital. She had a blood infection which took over her body, so she died. Brianna thinks that it is her fault that her mother didn't come home from the hospital." "That's so sad. Brianna is only three. Why does she think it's her fault." "I don't know, Sarah, but she really misses her mommy." "Maybe I could help her." "That's just what I was hoping you'd say!" "she really needs a special friend right now."

Sarah knew just what to do. She took Molly and went out into the hall. "Come on, Brianna, I want to show you my special place. Bring Max with you." Brianna and

Sarah ran out to the yard and sat under the dogwood tree. "This is my favorite spot because it is where I learned how to smile, and I think you will learn how to talk again too." Brianna listened attentively to Sarah, smiling and giggling at the same time. She really did want to talk again.

They began having tea parties with Molly, the rag doll, and Max the teddy. Slowly, one word at a time, Brianna began talking, and Sarah learned the importance of giggling. "Happiness sure is contagious!" Sarah chimed. "Me giggle too!" Brianna said with a gleam in her eye.

Sarah and Brianna became best friends and became known to all as the "giggle girls".

So the next time something sad happens in your family, or your friends' family, remember that you are not alone.

You can help each other in a way that will bring a new kind of happiness into your life. The girl without a voice taught Sarah how to giggle, and Sarah showed Brianna that it was okay for her to talk again.

Helping and being able to help is what makes life worth living. Don't ever give up, little one, you have friends you haven't even met yet!

CHAPTER 2

THE BEAUTY OF PATIENCE

It was early spring. The snow was almost gone and the flowers were beginning to spring up all over the meadow. The dew was dripping off the newly born leaves in the early morning sun. It was a beautiful day.

On a branch in a nearby apple tree, Katy caterpillar was awakened by a drop of dew that plopped on her nose. Katy opened her eyes and began to stretch as she realized Spring had finally come. Katy was very excited about Spring. A few months earlier her mother had told her of Gods' promise. She would one day become a beautiful butterfly. Katy longed to be beautiful. After all, she thought, who would pay any attention to a green caterpillar? I just look like a silly ol' worm, she thought. She struggled and struggled and pushed and pushed, but when she was done, all she had was a bruised belly.

"My goodness, she thought, becoming beautiful sure is hard work! I wonder how long this is going to take. Maybe God forgot me while I was sleeping!"

Katy's thoughts were interrupted by the happy sounds of field mice scampering in play on the ground below her. She decided to inch her way down to find out what made these mice so happy. It was a long walk, but she finally made it to the bottom.

"Hey!" she called, but her cry went unheard. "Hey!" she yelled a little louder. This time she got the attention of Mitsy and Carla. They were two of the happiest field mice she had ever seen.

"Who are you?" Mitsy asked. "My name is Katy." "What do you want from us?" asked Carla. "I...I... I was just wondering.... well.... why are you so happy?" "Aren't you happy?" "Not as happy as you two." "Why not?" "Well my mother told me that when Spring came I would be a beautiful butterfly. I tried and tried, but I'm still just a green caterpillar. What's wrong with me? Why can't I change and be happy like you? What's your secret?" "Well", said Mitsy, "When we were born, our mother told us that we were destined for greatness." "We weren't sure what that meant at first, but mom always told us that we were special", Carla piped up. "But what makes you special?" Katy asked. "Because we are mice," Carla stated. "You've always been mice. Don't you want to be something beautiful?" "But we are beautiful,"

Mitsy and Carla replied together. "God made us mice because that's what he wanted us to be. We will always be mice. We are beautiful, because God made us. You see, it's not how you look on the outside, but how you feel about yourself on the inside that makes you beautiful. You have to learn to be happy with who you are. Do everything that you know how to do as a caterpillar, and believe that you are beautiful because God made you. If God wants you to be a butterfly someday, then you will be. First you have to be happy with who you are. You have to like yourself. Do you understand, Katy?" "I think so. I guess I was trying too hard. Thank you for stopping to talk to me, Mitsy and Carla. I'll just be the best caterpillar I can be."

"That's the spirit!" the mice rang in together.

Mitsy and Carla went back to playing their games, and Katy made the long trek back up the tree. 'I wonder how much longer it will be,' she thought to herself.

A few weeks later Mitsy and Carla were playing under the same apple tree. They wondered how Katy was doing. Just then the most beautiful butterfly landed on the rock in front of them. "Hi Carla, hi Mitsy. Remember me?" "Katy? Is that you?" "Yes, it's me. How do I look?" "You're beautiful with all of your many colors." "You were right. Real beauty comes from within. I didn't change on the outside until I was happy with who I was on the inside. God made the changes, but not until he knew I was ready for them. Growing up happens, but it will happen at just the right time for you."

"How right you are, Katy. Let's all go play and enjoy our great big beautiful world!"

Carla, Mitsy, and Katy went off together, to enjoy the lives they had been given and they did their best to make others happy and help them realize their own potential.

CHAPTER 3

OBEDIENCE PAYS OFF

Jaimie, Jody, Julius, and Josie were a family of beavers who lived in the bog. The bog was surrounded by lots of trees and all the woodland creatures you could imagine. There were Henrietta and Arlo, the happy hares, Hop-a-long the pesky tree frog, Leaping Lily the grasshopper, Dan and Darla, the chattering chipmunks, and Felicity, a brand new baby fawn.

It was fall now and all the woodland creatures were preparing for the winter. The squirrels, Mr. and Mrs. Gray, were scrounging for nuts, as were Dan and Darla. There seemed to be a lot of nuts now, but who knew how long they would last.

Back at the bog, Jaimie and Jody were busy constructing a dam while their twin beavers, Julius and Josie were playing with sticks and leaves that had been collected. They were supposed to be helping, but it was more fun to play. "Josie, Julius!" yelled their mother.

"Where are you?" "Over here, mom!" Julius and Josie yelled together. "We're playing in the stack of twigs." "You're not supposed to be playing children, you're supposed to be helping us gather sticks to build one final dam before winter sets in. Then we have to make sure our house is sturdy enough to last the winter. When the work is done you may play. Let's get to work now." "Okay dad, we're coming." "Let's go Josie, the sooner we're done, the sooner we can play."

Julius and Josie darted off to find more twigs, but as usual they were distracted by the other woodland creatures and forgot what they were supposed to be doing. They came across Dan and Darla as they ran through the woods. "Hey Darla, want to play with us?" "Sorry, Josie, we have to collect nuts for the winter." "Okay. See you later!" Julius and Josie continued on their way until they came upon Henrietta and Arlo, the hares. They seemed to be busy as well, trying to get ready for winter. They were raking leaves and trying to clean things up around the outside of their house. "Want to play a game with us?" the beavers called. "We can't kids, we have too much work to do before the sun goes down." "Boy, Josie, no one wants to play with us," Julius said. "I know. Maybe dad was right." "What do you mean?" "Well, maybe we are supposed to get our work done first, and then play." "Yeh, and it's getting dark, so maybe we should go back." "Okay, Julius, let's go. I hope we're not in trouble!"

As they reached the front yard, mom and dad were still outside. "Oh no. Do you think they were looking for us?" "I don't know, but we better pick up some sticks to bring to them."

Just then dad saw them. "Where in the world have you two been? You were supposed to be helping us." "I'm sorry, dad, we stopped to talk to Dan and Darla and lost track of the time." "Well it's time to get cleaned up for supper and then bed. There will be no more playing today. Tomorrow will be a new day and we will begin by finishing the job we started today. There will be no playtime until it is done. Do you understand?" "Yes dad, I understand," whined Josie. "Julius?" "Yes, dad, I understand." "Good. Now get cleaned up!" Dad turned and began to walk away. "Dad?" called Julius, with tears in his eyes. "Yes, Julius? What is it?" "I was just wondering. Do you still love us?" "Do I still love you? Of course I still love you! Julius, Josie, come here and sit by me. Julius and Josie came and sat near their dad and listened intently to what he said. "There is nothing that you can do that will ever make me stop loving you. You are my children and I will always love you. You do need to understand one thing, though." "What's that dad?" "I need you to understand that I know what's best for you, and when I make a rule, it's for your own good. Do you understand this?" "Yes, dad." "How about you, Josie?"

"Yes, dad, I do understand."

"Okay then, please don't ever forget that I will always love you both." "We won't daddy," Julius and Josie cried together. "We love you too!" And with that, they gave their dad the biggest hug they had ever given him. "From now on we will listen and be good." Jaimie hugged both of his children as tight as he could.

The next day they helped their parents finish getting ready for winter, and continued enjoying playing in the woods until the snow came.

CHAPTER 4

THE TRUE MEANING OF FRIENDSHIP

It had been a long, tough winter. Derrick knew that everything would be okay. Patty wasn't so sure. She was a worrier. "What if we run out of money, or don't have enough food to eat?" she thought. These were big problems for a six year old. Patty tried to sleep that night, but she kept thinking about what might happen. "Maybe I should find a job to help out. I can sell newspapers, or my toys," she thought.

The night was long. Patty got up with a stomach ache, so her mom kept her home from school. Derrick left for school at 8:30 sharp. He met Peter and Meg in the school yard. "Where's Patty?" "She stayed home with a stomach ache." "I hope she's okay." said Meg. "She will be after she rests."

Back at home Patty talked to her mother. "What if daddy doesn't get better? What if he can't ever go back to work?" "Patty, my dear child, you shouldn't be worried about these things." "I can't help it mommy. What if we run out of food?" "God will take care of us Patty." "I know, but I'd feel better if our refrigerator were full." "As long as your stomach is full, that's all that matters." "I guess so." "Okay little miss worrier, get some rest. I'll check on you later."

While Patty slept, Mrs. Pratt checked on her husband. Mr. Pratt had a problem with his blood, and the doctors still hadn't found the right medication. He felt a little better today and he ate a small breakfast. This was good, because he had lost a lot of weight since he first became ill. He wasn't much more than skin and bones.

When Patty woke up, she found her dad sitting in the stuffed chair in the living room. She climbed up into his lap and gave him a hug. "Are you okay, Daddy?" "I'm still sick, "Muffin," but I do feel better today." "Are we going to run out of money, Daddy?" "What? Where did you get that idea?" "I was just thinking, that's all." If we need money, I could sell my toys." "You don't have to sell your toys, Patty. We haven't run out of money, yet, and we will always have enough food to eat. You, my dear, are much too young to be worried about such things. Is Derrick worried too?" "No. He said everything would be okay, but I didn't believe him." "Well, he's right. Everything will be okay, so you don't have to worry anymore." "I'll try not to, but sometimes it's hard." "I know."

Later in the day, Derrick came home with Peter and Meg. "How is Patty, Mom?" "She feels a lot better than she did this morning." "Let's go see her!" "Hi, Patty! How are you?" "I'm okay, now. My stomach doesn't hurt anymore." "That's good. We really missed you at school today." "Thanks, I'll be there tomorrow!"

Just then there was a knock at the door. "I'll get it!" shouted Derrick. He opened the door to find a tall man in a three piece suit. "Hi, sonny. Is your father home?" "He's sick. I'll get my mom." Mrs. Pratt came to the door. "Hi. May I help you?"

"Yes, mam. I'm Mr. Saunders, the president of Jason Enterprises. We know how sick your husband has been so we took up a collection. We hope this helps until he can return to work."

"Thank you so much! You'll never know how much this means!"

Patty, sitting in the background, listened to all that was said. "Wow!" she thought to herself. "Now I know for sure that everything will be okay!" Her stomach ache was gone for good and she did not have to sell her toys!

CHAPTER 5

MY BEST FRIEND WAS A CAT. OR: THE LIFE AND TIMES OF MORRIS

Once upon a time, on a small farm in Maine, there lived a cat named Morris. He probably should've been named "Mischief" because of all the trouble he got into. He never got into any real trouble, he really just wanted lots of attention and would do anything to get it. Morris was an indoor cat and very afraid of loud noises. He hid when a garbage truck came down the street, or when he heard sirens.

Morris's owner, was a single lady who lived alone. Her name was Pam and she loved Morris. Morris followed Pam everywhere except outside. If Pam was watching television Morris was sure to be on her lap. One day while Pam sat at her kitchen table writing a letter, Morris jumped up on the table and laid himself down in the middle of her letter! "What are you doing, Morris? Are you looking for attention by any chance?" Pam asked her purring Kitty. "You sure do like being treated like a king!" He certainly was in his glory when he was the center of attention, which was most of the time.

In many ways, Morris was just like other cats with some very silly antics. He would jump in and out of boxes and bags, and chase bugs across the floor. One day he wanted to see what was in a rather small bag. He got his head in but he couldn't get it out! After she stopped laughing, Pam pulled the bag off his head.

Morris was also like a child in many ways. He always played with his food. He would take the dry food, a piece at a time, throw it up in the air, jump up and pounce on it. He did this several times before actually eating it. Morris had other talents as well. For instance, he enjoyed helping Pam cook. He would always be up on the counter in the middle of whatever she was doing. He loved raw spaghetti. He didn't eat it. He played with it until he got bored! One time while he was on the counter, he began wagging his tail. What he didn't know was that he was wagging it in and out of the flame under a pot on the stove. Pam didn't know either until a funny smell reached her nose. You can imagine what happened next. Pam went one way and the cat went the other! Morris wasn't hurt, thank heavens. Just the hairs on the end of his tail were singed slightly. There were a lot of close calls, but it didn't matter because Morris and Pam were best friends. They kept each other company and warm on those cold winter nights. Morris not only slept in the same bed with Pam, but he would get under the covers, all the way down to the end of the bed and sleep next to her feet. On another occasion, Pam had just gotten comfortable (OOPS!) UNDER THE COVERS, when there was a tremendous crash in another room that shook the whole apartment. Pam turned on the light, crawled out of bed, and went to see what had happened. In the bathroom she found the sink laying on the floor! Morris had jumped on it, as he always did, to get water from the faucet, or to jump from the sink to the window. This time was different, however, the sink did not hold him! Fortunately, he was not hurt, and he decided it was much safer to get into bed with his mistress.

Although Morris was an indoor cat, during the nice weather he ventured outside, but stayed very close to his mistress. He had no desire to go near the street because of his fear of loud noises. During the summer, Pam had trouble getting him back inside. He was having too much fun chasing all those bugs!

These are just a few of the antics of Morris during the few years he lived with Pam. The day eventually came when Pam had to move. Unfortunately, she couldn't take Morris to the new house with her. It was a sad day indeed, but Morris still lives on a farm in Maine with a family who needs him. Pam misses him, but he is loved and in very good hands; and according to Morris: so are the bugs! (in good paws that is!)

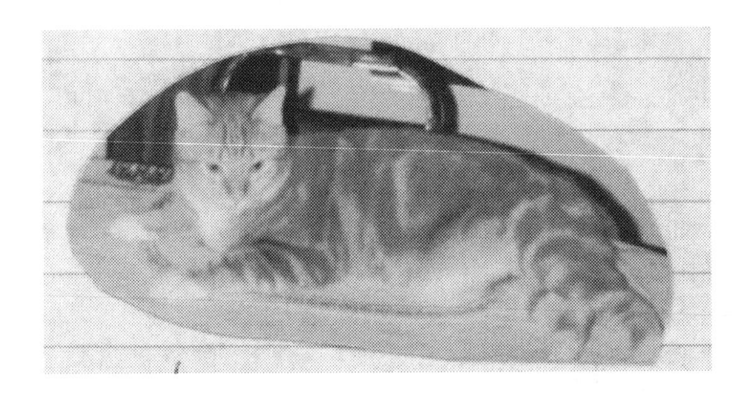

This is Morris!

CHAPTER 6

THE IMPORTANCE OF SHARING FEELINGS

Randy and Rachel lived in the same neighborhood. They played games together both inside and outside.

"Sometimes I wonder if they're not spending too much time together," said Mrs. Brown, Rachel's mother. "They play well together," agreed Mrs. Andrews, "because they are the same age, but they should have some other friends." I'm sure they will in time."

Just then there was a scream from the backyard. Both mothers went running to see what had happened. As they approached the backyard Randy was standing in the middle of the sandbox, while Rachel sat on the ground crying. "Randy? What happened to Rachel?" "I don't know mommy. We were building a castle and all of a sudden she threw down her shovel and screamed." Mrs. Brown knelt down on the ground by Rachel to see if she was hurt. "No, mommy, I'm just mad." "Why, Rachel? Did Randy do something to you?" "He made me mad because he wouldn't do what I wanted him to." "I see. You got mad at Randy because you couldn't have your own way." "My way was better mommy, but Randy wouldn't listen to me." "When you play with someone each of you has to give a little. That's called compromise," said Mrs. Andrews. "Yes," Mrs. Brown agreed, "You must be willing to share ideas." "That's right, Mrs. Brown, and I bet they could make a wonderful sand castle if they share ideas, and do a little bit of what each one wants."

"I'm sorry, mommy." "You know I love you Rachel, but you should say you're sorry to Randy." "Do I have to?" "Yes, Rachel." "Okay I will." "I'm sorry I got mad at you Randy. I didn't mean to hurt your feelings." "That's okay, Rachel, I'm still your friend." "I hope so."

"Okay, how about you two starting over, and we'll come back and see your castle when you're done," said Mrs. Andrews.

"Good idea", agreed Mrs. Brown. "We'll go inside while you work, and you can come get us when you're done." "Okay, we will." Mrs. Brown and Mrs. Andrews went back inside to finish their tea.

"Let's build the best sand castle ever, Rachel." "Okay Randy, How about both of us getting buckets of sand to add? We could each get the same number of buckets

and then decide together how to add them to our castle."
"That sounds good to me, Rachel."

So Rachel and Randy filled their buckets with sand, and worked together to make the best castle ever. Later that day their moms came outside to see their castle and took a picture of it so that they could always remember it.

All of this happened late in the summer and it was soon time for the children to get ready for school. They would both be in the first grade this year. The Saturday before school was to start, was designated the day to buy school clothes. Randy went with his mom to "kids town". He bought two new pairs of jeans, and two new cowboy shirts. He also got socks, underwear, new shoes and a pair of cowboy boots.

Rachel went with her mom to "Girls are us" to shop. She got a pair of pink slacks, a Barbie blouse, a Barbie sweatshirt, and Barbie sneakers. She also got a couple of corduroy jumpers, socks and underwear. Later in the day, Rachel and her mom met Randy and his mom for lunch at Jack-in-the-box.

"How's the shopping going," asked Mrs. Andrews. "I think we have all the clothes Rachel needs to start school" replied Mrs. Brown. "Randy is all set too. We just need to get a lunchbox and pencils and crayons." "Rachel needs a lunchbox too, so maybe we could go to Paperama together. Everything costs less there."

"That's a good idea."

"Okay, kids, what's for lunch?" "I want a burger and fries said Randy, "and a glass of coke." "Me too," said Rachel.

"A burger, fries, and a coke it is," said Mrs. Brown.

"I'm having a salad and coffee, how about you, Mrs. Brown?"

"That sounds good to me." "Okay everybody, let's dig in!"

After everyone had their fill, they headed for Paperama.

When they went inside, they found two shelves of lunch boxes. Randy picked out the Indiana Jones one, and Rachel wanted the Barbie one, of course. Next they went to look for crayons, pencils and pencil boxes. They each found a box of crayons, and pencils with their names on them. Randy found a pencil box with the Ninja turtles, and Rachel found one with Goldilocks and the three bears.

"Well kids, that should do it! You've got everything you need for the first day of school." Mrs. Brown said.

"Let's go home. It's been a long day, and my feet are tired" said Mrs. Andrews.

On the way home Randy and Rachel talked excitedly about school. "I hope we have the same teacher, Randy." "Me too, Rachel. That way we would both have at least one friend to start school with." "You're both going to make new friends in school, even if you don't end up in the same class." "I know, but it would be so much fun to be together."

Well, the first day of school finally came and off they went, lunchboxes in hand. As it turned out, Rachel was in Mrs. Jones' class, and Randy was in Miss Johnson's class. Rachel was upset at first, but at lunch she sat with a girl named Crystal. Crystal was in her class and lived a few streets away from Rachel. Randy made friends with a boy named Jason at lunch. Jason lives on the same street as Crystal and the four of them became good friends.

When Randy and Rachel returned home they were all excited about school and the friends they had made. School was a good experience for them.

They learned how to write their names, and all the letters of the alphabet. They also learned new songs and games, and how to share their feelings with others. They found out it was just as okay to be angry or sad, as it is to be happy and glad. They also found out that they always had someone to talk to about their feelings. That was most important of all.

CHAPTER 7

JUST ANOTHER DAY DOWN ON THE FARM: E.I.E.I.O.

"Cock-a-doodle-doo!" shouted Robbie Rooster. Robin Redbreast sang a beautiful song in a nearby apple tree. The sun had just come up and it was time to feed the animals.

Farmer John rubbed his eyes and rolled out of bed. It was hard to come out from under the covers on cool mornings like this one. It was the middle of November and almost all of the leaves were on the ground. "I'm getting too old for this routine," sighed Farmer John as he pulled on his overalls. "Oh well, time to milk the cows."

Out in the barn the cows were mooing loudly. "Okay, okay girls, I'm coming. You're first, Bessy." Bucket in hand, Farmer John sat on his three-legged stool and began squirting milk into his bucket. Swish, swish, swish, swish. "There! Now it's your turn, Edna." Swish, swish, swish,

swish. While Farmer John milked the cows, his wife, Charlotte, fed the chickens and collected the eggs.

"Don't forget, John, today's the day that fifteen preschoolers are coming to visit our farm." "I haven't forgotten, dear. After breakfast, I'll get the ponies ready. Molly and Muscles are just the right size for the children to ride." "Come in to eat as soon as you can, dear." "I will, I'm almost done here."

A few minutes later, Farmer John entered the kitchen with two buckets of fresh milk. He placed them on the counter and washed up to eat. Charlotte had prepared eggs, sausages, toast, and a fresh pot of coffee. "Boy am I hungry! I always work up an appetite first thing in the morning!" "Well, there's plenty, so eat up. You'll need the strength when the children are here." "Yes dear." Charlotte had eaten earlier, so while John ate, she fed Major, a very special year old collie, and the three cats: Muffin, Puffin and Stuffin. Major thought he was in charge of the farm. He was indeed a very good watchdog. The cats, however, thought they were the most important animals on the farm. After all, they were the prettiest!

With breakfast dishes washed and put away, Charlotte began preparing goodies for the children who were to arrive at ten o'clock. John went back out to the barn to put saddles on Molly and Muscles. He then took them out to the pasture where they could graze.

Farmer John was busy stacking hay when the bus drove up the dirt driveway. By this time, the cows were out grazing, as well as the rest of the horses, and the chickens were running around the fenced in yard. As the bus got closer, Charlotte came outside to greet the excited children. John also, stopped stacking hay, to help give the guided tour.

Mrs. Thatcher got off the bus and guided fifteen very excited children, (3&4 yr. olds) down the stairs. Her class aides, Miss Jean, and Miss Paula, also came to help out.

"Well, hello there, everyone! I'm Farmer John, and this is my wife, Miss Charlotte." "Hi, Farmer John. Thank you so much for letting us come to visit your farm." "It's our pleasure. Okay everyone, follow me into the barn."

Once everyone was in the barn, Farmer John showed the children how he stacks the hay. "That sure is a lot of hay, isn't it?" Miss Paula noted. "What's the hay for?" asked four year old Brandon. It's food for the horses and cows. "Can we see what it tastes like?" "No Brandon, because if we eat the hay, we'll get sick." replied Farmer John. "Don't worry, Brandon, we have a special surprise for all of you to take back to the school." Charlotte said.

"Okay, I guess I won't eat the hay." replied Brandon.

"Now let's go see how sadie and her piglets are doing."

In a stall way at the back of the barn, was Sadie, a very large, very pink pig, with her eight little piglets. "Aren't they cute?" asked Miss Jean. "Can we hold them?" Molly wanted to know. "No," Miss Charlotte answered, "But I will pick one up and let you pat it." "Me first!" "No, me!" "Don't push, children, you will all get a turn.

Once everyone had a turn, the piglet was returned to his mother and the tour continued.

"Okay, everyone, who wants a pony ride?" asked farmer John. "Me!" "Me!" all the children shouted together. "Let's go to the pasture. The horses are ready and waiting."

One by one Miss Charlotte and Farmer John took the children around the pasture on the ponies until everyone had a turn. While they rode the ponies, they saw the chickens running around, and the cows grazing in the field. Major, who thought he was in charge, and the three cats, Muffin, Puffin, and Stuffin, were running around in the middle of everything. After the last child had had his ride on the ponies, Miss Charlotte had everyone wait on the porch while she went inside to get the surprise. She came back out with freshly baked gingerbread, and chocolate chip cookies. "Here are some goodies to take back to school with you," Mrs. Thatcher. "Thank you, so much! Let's all thank Farmer John and Miss Charlotte for the tour and the goodies, children." "Thank you Farmer John!" all the children shouted at once. "Okay, let's all get back on the bus. It's time to go back to school." "Do we have to? I want to stay here and have fun!" "Me too!" "Sorry kids, we really do have to go."

Mrs. Thatcher, Miss Jean, and Miss Paula got everyone on the bus and buckled in. As they drove down the driveway, Farmer John and Charlotte heard the children singing at the top of their lungs: "Old MacDonald had a farm, E.I.E.I.O.!"

CHAPTER 8

BONNIE BUNNY'S HELPING HAND

It was late October and the tree outside Bonnie Bunny's kitchen window was almost bare. Robin Redbreast was sitting on a branch singing her heart out as the last two leaves fell. "Hmm", Bonnie thought, "Pretty soon I'll have to keep this window closed. I won't be able to hear Robin's beautiful song. I sure do miss the birds during winter. Their songs are so pretty.

Today was one of her busiest days. She was making pies for the harvest ball, held every year on Halloween night. So far she had made one gooseberry, one pumpkin, and one mince pie. She put them on the window sill to cool, and as she put the third one down, she saw terrible Barney Bunny running away with one of her pies. "You get back here right now with that pie!" she screamed out the window. "I put way too much work into my pies to have them stolen by the neighborhood troublemaker!"

She thought to herself. Somebody ought to teach that boy manners. Her children, Martha and Mitchel, were whispering in the doorway. Henrietta the mouse was in the doorway with them, waiting for her chance at the pies. The mouse had lived in the hole in the wall for so long that the children gave her a name.

"So, Mitchell, what do you think? Should we tell Mom the whole story?" "I don't know," he said. "She might get angrier." "But it's not Barney's fault that he had to steal the pie." "Okay, let's go tell her now." "Mother? Can we talk to you? It's about Barney." "He's a troublemaker!" snapped mom. "He has a problem we need to tell you about." said Mitchel. "He doesn't get much food at home. He doesn't have a dad, and his mother lost her job because she had to take too many days off from work when she was sick during the summer." "Have you met Barney's mother?" "Yes," said Martha. "We walked him home from the park one day and introduced ourselves to her. She seemed very nice, but she makes Barney stay out of the house during the day, except to eat and use the bathroom. She doesn't have the energy to keep up with him. She gives him as much food as she can, but often he goes without breakfast, and sometimes supper too. When we were out playing this morning, we found him out behind the shed, crying. He said he was hungry. He didn't have any supper last night, and breakfast was one slice of toast." "Is it really that bad," asked mom. "Yes, mom, it is," said Mitchell.

"Oh, Mother," cried Martha, is their anything we can do for them? I know it wasn't right for him to steal the pie, but he is really desperate, and very hungry."

"Okay, children, calm down," Mother said. "Let me finish the pies and then you can show me where they live. Meanwhile, out in the shed are some boxes. Each of you bring one in. We'll fill them with canned goods, bread, cereal, fruit, and other things to help them." "Thanks, Mom," Mitchell said, and Martha hugged her. "We'll be right back!"

Mother finished baking the last of her pies, while the children began filling the boxes with all kinds of good things. "Let's use your wagon for the boxes," Martha suggested. "These sure are heavy," said Martha. "That's because there's so much good food in them!" said Mitchell. "Okay, I'm just taking the last pie out of the oven now." Bonnie took off her apron and grabbed a sweater. "Let's get going."

They followed the path up a steep hill. Mitchell pulled the wagon and Martha pushed it from behind.

It was a tough climb, but they finally made it to the top. It was so much easier going down the other side. At the bottom of the hill was a little farm house with a tire hanging from a tree in the front yard. "Hi Barney, we have some food for you. Can I go in and see your mom?" asked Bonnie. "Sure, I'll tell her you're here." Barney ran inside, and was back in a flash. "My mother's awake and wants you to come in." Mitchell and Barney carried one box in, and Martha helped her mom with the other one. "Hi, my name is Bonnie. Sorry to just drop in on you. I know you haven't felt well." "That's okay, Bonnie. I could use the company. My name is Emily. I'm glad Barney finally has friends to play with." "Barney's welcome to come to our house any time, and so are you, Emily. If there is ever anything I can do to help you, please ask. We've brought you some food to help you get through the rest of the month. Please don't ever feel you have to go hungry. There are always people around who are willing to help."

"Thank you so much, Bonnie. I really appreciate what you've done for us."

From that day on, Emily got better and better. She eventually was able to return to work. Barney apologized to Bonnie for stealing the pie, and promised never to steal again.

On the way home that day, Bonnie told Martha and Mitchell how proud she was of them, and gave them each a big hug. Bonnie and Emily became good friends, and Martha, Mitchell and Barney became best friends and did everything together from that day on.

CHAPTER 9

REAL LIFE OR FANTASY

Sometimes you just have to cry. The worst part is that most of the time, no one hears you. You are alone with your tears. This is the way it was with Janice. She was one of three children and very seldom noticed. Oh, she was clothed and fed, and went to school, but no one paid any attention to her, or so she thought. She had friends at school, but no one ever came to her house to play with her, so she immersed herself in books. She pretty much lived in a fantasy world. She even had a fantasy family: one that paid attention to her.

One day she was out in the backyard laying on the grass. She was in the middle of one of her fantasies: "Hi, mom, it's me, Janice." "Hi, Janice, how are you today?" "I'm fine, but I wish you weren't just a doll." "Me too, Janice, then I could hug you." "That would be wonderful, but this is only make believe."

Just then her mom came out to find her. "Who are you talking to, Janice?" "I was talking to my imaginary mom." "Why do you need an imaginary mom when you have a real mom?" "I'm sorry, mom, but you never pay any attention to me. Sometimes I need someone to talk to." "What do you mean, Janice? I love you." "I know, but you never have time for me. You're either taking Becky to her basketball games, or Rodney to Cub Scouts. You never take me anywhere." "That's because you're only six, and not old enough yet to play sports or be in clubs. When you are seven, you will be old enough to join the Blue Birds, but until then, you'll have to wait." "That seems so far away!" "I know, but maybe we can spend one afternoon a week together. You can invite your friends over after school and have a reading club or something. I'll make cookies and lemonade and you could all share your favorite books with each other." "That sounds good. What day should we do it?" "I think Friday would be the best for me, but I'll check with the other parents. Who do you want to come?"

"I want Lisa, Penny, Tammy, Sheri, and Susie." "That sounds like a good group to me. Let's go in and call everyone." "Okay, mom, I'll put my doll away for now."

Mrs. Jones made all of the calls, and all of the parents agreed that this was a great idea. The first meeting was to be held on Friday, at the picnic table in the Jones' back yard.

When Friday came all of the children couldn't wait for school to get out. Some of them sat together at lunch. "I can't wait for the meeting today, Janice!" "Me too! I'm bringing three books." "Which ones are you bringing, Lisa?" "I'm bringing: WINNIE THE POOH, BRAER RABBIT, and CURIOUS GEORGE." "Oh boy, I love those books!" said Sheri. "What about you, Tammy?" "Well, I think I'm bringing: THE VELVETEEN RABBIT, DUMBO, and the THREE BEARS." "I can't wait!" said Janice. "We are going to have so much fun!" "We better hurry and eat lunch, here comes Mrs. Thompson." "Hi, girls. I hope everyone is eating their lunch!" "We are, Mrs. Thompson." "Lunch is almost over, girls, so don't play." "We won't!"

Lunch was soon over, but school couldn't end soon enough for the girls. Three O'clock finally came, and the girls hurried home to change into play clothes. They got their books together and headed for Janice's house. When they arrived, Janice was at the picnic table with Susie. She had come earlier with her mom because she was in a wheelchair. This was her first time in a long time going to a friends house, and she was excited to be there. When the rest of the girls arrived, the yard was filled with squeels and giggles. Mrs. Jones came out with the cookies and lemonade while the girls gathered around Susie. "Come eat your snack girls.

Leave your books on the grass for now, so you don't spill on them" Once settled at the table, Mrs. Jones passed the plate of cookies. "Please take two cookies, and I will pour your drinks." While they were eating, they were full of chatter about school and their books. When they had finished eating, they cleaned the table, putting their cups and napkins in the barrel at the end of the driveway.

They decided to spread a blanket on the grass to sit on. Susie was very tiny, so Mrs. Jones picked her up and sat her on the blanket with the others. They had a good variety of books to share and Mrs. Jones read some of them to the girls because they hadn't learned to read yet. She read: SAMMY THE SEAL, LITTLE RED RIDING HOOD, THE TALES OF PETER RABBIT, and CURIOUS GEORGE GOES TO THE HOSPITAL. When they were through looking at the books, they put them on the picnic table and played a few games. Mrs. Jones put Susie back in her chair. They played RED ROVER, RED ROVER, and Old lady witch. They also played jump rope for a while. The afternoon went fast, and soon it was time for the girls to go home. Susie's mom came to get her, and Mrs. Jones brought the others home. They had such a good time that they decided to meet at a different house each week. Next week, the meeting would be at Susie's.

When Janice went to bed that night, she thanked her mom, and gave her a big hug. She also told her mom that she didn't need a fantasy mom any more, because she had the best mom there was. She realized that she really did have friends and they were very good friends indeed!

CHAPTER 10

THE MISADVENTURES OF WADDLES

Waddles the duck, lived in the zoo with Bundles, a polar bear cub, Ollie the ostrich, Kelly the kangaroo, and Sammy the seal. There were a lot of animals in the zoo, but these were the ones most familiar to Waddles. Now Waddles, was a very social duck and made friends with everyone, but he had one problem. He always seemed to be in trouble. For instance, just the other day Waddles was wandering around his pen when he noticed a hole in the ground. He got real close and looked in, but it was too dark for him to see anything. He just had to know what was in that hole, so he pushed his head all the way in the hole. He still couldn't see, but now he was in trouble. His head was stuck! He wiggled and wiggled, flapping his wings, but he was just plain stuck! Not far away, Shelby, a six year old, was visiting the zoo with her mother. She happened to notice Waddles' predicament, so she got her mother. Her mother went to find the zoo keeper. "My, my!" said Mr. Lambert. "You just can't stay out of trouble, can you, Waddles?" Mr. Lambert gently placed his hands around Waddles' neck and pulled him to safety. "You know Waddles, that's what happens when you stick your nose where it doesn't belong! You're just lucky that Mr. gopher didn't come and bite your bill!" Mr. Lambert chuckled. Shelby patted Waddles and gave him a big hug. "There, now!" she said, "You're okay."

Waddles just walked away with his head held high, as if nothing had happened.

Then there was the time when Waddles decided to challenge Ollie the ostrich. He had gotten into the ostrich pen and decided to snack on the food left in the bin. Ollie would have none of that, so he went after the intruder.

He gave him a nudge from behind, but Waddles didn't budge. He was a stubborn duck. He had no idea who he was dealing with. Ollie nudged him again, this time much harder. Waddles jumped and started to move out of the way. He decided to try again, however, and this time Ollie took a nip at him. Well, Waddles didn't like this at all and started squawking loudly, until Mr. Lambert came and got him out of the pen. Waddles loved to get into things but he was really just curious. He was always afraid he might miss something. He didn't want anyone to have fun without him!

One day he saw Bundles and Boxer, the two polar bear cubs, playing together. Of course he wanted to be in the middle!

"Hey, Bundles, what game are you playing?" "We're playing catch with a rubber ball." "Can I play?" asked Waddles. "I don't think so Waddles, you don't have any hands. You can't catch with your wings." "Maybe I could catch with my beak. Please let me try." "Okay, if you can find a way in here, we'll let you try." Waddles was trying to dig his way under the fence, when John, Mr. Lambert's helper, came up behind him. "Well, what do we have here?" asked John. "Don't you think you should play with the other ducks instead of the bears?" "I don't have any fun with those ducks!" replied Waddles. "All they do is swim and fly around the pond. I'll have more fun with the bears." "Come on, Waddles, Let's go back to the pond." "Oh, alright. See you later, Bundles." "Okay, Waddles!" Waddles went back to the pond, but he sure was itching to get into trouble. What can I do now, thought Waddles. I can't seem to do much without getting caught. He somehow managed to stay out of trouble for the rest of the day. There's always tomorrow, he thought. He'd visit Sammy the seal, after breakfast.

The sun came up bright and early the next day and Waddles waited patiently for his breakfast. Surprisingly, Waddles stayed in his own area. He didn't bother anyone while they were eating.

"Well, Waddles, I see you've learned some manners after all. It's nice to see you eating your own food for once." What John didn't know, was that Waddles had plans to visit others later in the day. He kept his cool though, so no one would know his plans ahead of time. After all the animals had been fed, John and Mr. Lambert went about their daily routines to get ready for the children that would soon arrive. This was Waddles chance. As soon as John and Mr. Lambert were out of view, Waddles began inching his way up to where the seals were. As he waddled up the dirt path, the bears yelled out to him. "Good morning, Waddles!" "Good morning, bears," he whispered. "Shh. Please keep your voices down, or I'll get caught!" As he kept waddling, he went by Ollie the ostrich. "Hi Waddles!" squawked Ollie. "What kind of trouble will you get into today?"

I'm not looking for trouble. I just want to visit Sammy and Sara for a while." "Well get along then." "Bye, Ollie!" Waddles then passed the giraffes, the deer pen and the sheep. Finally, he reached the seals. "Hi Sammy, hi Sara." Waddles called out. "Hi, Waddles, how are you today?" "Just fine, thanks. I thought I'd come and visit you for a while." "We're always glad to have the company, but I hope you don't get into trouble again." "Aw, I'm not worried. I can't get into trouble for talking to you. I only get into trouble when I manage to get into the pens."

"Well, just in case, we should keep an eye out for old Mr. Lambert and John."

Just then John came up behind Waddles. "And what have we here?" "I'm just talking to Sammy and Sara, John. I won't try to get into the pen." "Well, see that you don't. You've been in quite enough trouble for one week!" "Okay, okay, I'll do my best to stay out of trouble," Waddles replied. "We'll see!" said John as he went on his way.

Waddles kept his word and did not cause any problems at all that morning. At lunch time, he went back to his pen, and ate like a gentleman. "I'm proud of you Waddles, you really kept your word this morning!" Mr. Lambert noticed. "Thank you for noticing! I hope it's okay for me to visit Bundles and Boxer this afternoon. I think those baby polar bears are so cute!" "It's okay, as long as you stay out side their pen." "I will."

To everyone's surprise, Waddles stayed out of trouble all day long! He had a good day, and tired himself out. He stayed in his pen and slept all night. When the sun came up the next day, Waddles woke up fully rested. When Mr. Lambert came to the ducks pen, Waddles was waiting patiently. "Well Waddles, this is going to be a good day for you!" "It is? Why?" "Because a new duck is coming to join you, Hillary, and Henry." "Really?" "Yes, her name is Wanda." "Oh boy, I can't wait to meet her! I'll stay here after breakfast to wait for her." "That sounds like a good idea, Waddles, I'll see you after breakfast." Mr. Lambert left to feed the rest of the animals, and Waddles ate his breakfast with much excitement about meeting someone new.

Wanda arrived just before lunch. Waddles fell in love the minute he saw her. She is the most beautiful duck I've ever seen, thought Waddles to himself. After lunch, he took Wanda around the zoo to introduce her to all the animals. After this, they went back to their own area and spent the rest of the day getting to know each other. Mr. Lambert and John watched them from a distance.

"Well!" said John, "I think we've found the answer to the "Waddles" problem!" "Yes, I agree," replied Mr. Lambert. "I think Wanda will do a good job of keeping Waddles out of trouble from now on!"

Mr. Lambert and John were right. Waddles and Wanda did everything together and became good friends. Waddles was no longer the uncoordinated, mischievous duck that everyone once knew.

I LOVE YOU

A PERSONAL NOTE FROM THE AUTHOR

All of the stories in this book have been a part of my life in some way. I love the Lord with all my heart, because He is the one who has made the difference in my life. He has always been there, even though there were times when I didn't recognize His presence. Especially during the tough times! I would not know how special I am, or how much I am loved, if I did not know the Lord. I would also not know how much I could accomplish with His help, unless some very good friends had told me and daily encourage me to keep growing.

I am very thankful to all of those who had a part in making this book possible. I thank the Lord for giving me the words to say, and for helping me conquer my fear of failure.

Please read the following with an open heart:

GOD'S TIMING

As I sit here waiting for that all important telephone call, I wonder: Did I get the job?

When will they have a car for me?

Does anyone else struggle like me?

How much longer will I have to wait?

Does God really care? Where is He anyway?

Why can't just one transition in my life go smoothly?

Then I remember God's Word:

PSALM 31:15: "My times are in your hands, O Lord."

JEREMIAH 29:11: "I know the plans I have for you. Plans for hope and a future."

ROMANS 8:28: "All things work together for good to those who love God."

JOHN 16:33: "In this world you will have tribulation, be of good cheer, I have overcome the world."

ROMANS 8:37: "We are more than conquerors through Him that loved us."

ROMANS 8:39: "No one and nothing will ever be able to separate you from the love of God."

PHILIPPIANS 1:6: "He who began a good work in you, will bring it to completion."

HEBREWS 13:5: "I will never leave you nor forsake you."

NEHEMIAH 8:10: "The joy of the Lord is your strength."

PHILIPPIANS 4:13: "I can do all things through Christ who gives me the strength."{Most of the scripture verses are from the N.I.V.}

2 CORINTHIANS 12:9,10: "My grace is sufficient for you, for my strength is made perfect in weakness. For when I am weak, then am I strong."

1 CORINTHIANS 10:13: "I will never give you anything that you cannot bear. I will always provide a way out."

LUKE 12.7: "All the hairs on my head are numbered."

PSALM 139.16: "All the days of my life were written in your Book before I was even born."

ISAIAH 55.8: "My thoughts are not your thoughts, and my ways are not your ways," saith the Lord."

I know from experience that God's way is always best. He meets every need and answers every prayer at exactly the right time. For this reason I can sing with a grateful heart:

"Tis so sweet to trust in Jesus," and "I know who holds tomorrow."

I am encouraged as I am reminded that God also had to wait.

God sent His only Son, Jesus, to earth to show a bunch of misfits how to live. God had to watch and wait as His Son walked this earth showing us the proper way to live, and what it means to "Love your neighbor as yourself." God let His Son leave heaven to do this even though He knew what the end result would be.

Jesus would have to die the most horrible of deaths: death on a cross. God had to wait for His Son to return to heaven, and they both knew this could not happen until His mission was complete. He must take all of the sins of the world on Himself and die, in order that we, His creation might have life.

God loved us so much, that He was willing to turn His back on His own precious Son, while He died for us. God, in His perfection cannot look at sin, and for the moment that Jesus died, He had to look away. I can only imagine how much this must have hurt, but it was done out of love for you and me. Jesus loved His Father so much that He would've done anything He asked. God loved us so much that He willingly gave His only Son so that we could all be part of His family, if we want to. Jesus was the only perfect man, and He was God at the same time. How did He feel about those who pounded the spikes into His hands?

"Father forgive them, for they know not what they do!" Wow! Could I forgive someone who treated me or someone I knew that way? What if they killed you or I for doing what is right? Could we forgive them in that moment before we died?

Jesus died, and three days later, He rose from His grave, and a short time later, returned to heaven to sit at

His Father's right hand. It would seem that God no longer had to wait. He had His Son back so His wait was over, and His mission complete. Right? Wrong! God is still waiting! He is waiting for you and me. We must choose the kind of life we will live, and who we will serve. We must choose to accept this free gift of salvation, because God doesn't force Himself on us. Jesus paid the only price acceptable to God for our sins. He gave His life! ROMANS 6.23 says: "The wages of sin is death, but the gift of God is eternal life through Jesus Christ."

Is He waiting for you? Salvation is a gift, but unless it is accepted, it is of little or no value. I encourage you to accept this free gift today. It's just a matter of admitting that you have sinned and cannot save yourself. It's as simple as praying the following:

Dear Lord Jesus,

I know that I have sinned and cannot save myself.

Please forgive my sin, and live in my heart. Thank you, Jesus, for dying for me. Amen.

If you haven't given your life to the Lord already, I encourage you to do so. I also encourage you to find a church that will help you to grow spiritually. God bless you!

Because of Jesus, Faith

2 CORINTHIANS 6.2: "Today is the day of salvation. Now is the accepted hour."

Printed in the United States
By Bookmasters